KATIE'S WORLD

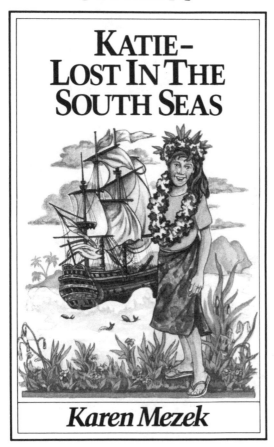

KATIE – LOST IN THE SOUTH SEAS

Karen Mezek

HARVEST HOUSE PUBLISHERS
Eugene, Oregon 97402

MRS. JULIA THOMPSEN

MR. JOHN McABE THOMPSEN

KATIE THOMPSEN

BETH McKINNEY

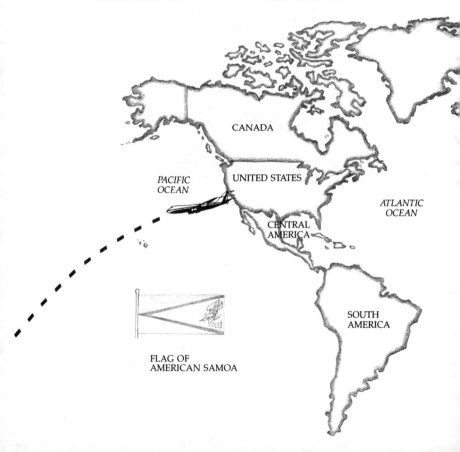

CANADA

UNITED STATES

PACIFIC OCEAN

CENTRAL AMERICA

ATLANTIC OCEAN

SOUTH AMERICA

FLAG OF AMERICAN SAMOA

GRANDPA THOMPSEN

BIG BLAKE

PETER THOMPSEN

KATIE—LOST IN THE SOUTH SEAS

Copyright © 1991 by Karen Mezek
Published by House Publishers
Eugene, Oregon 97402

Library of Congress Cataloging-in-Publication Data

Mezek, Karen, 1956-
    Katie—lost in the south seas   /   Karen Mezek.
    Summary: When her father goes to the South Seas to write about marauding pirates, Katie
accompanies him and has an adventure aboard a pirate ship.
    ISBN 0-89081-900-9
    [1. Pirates—Fiction.]   I. Title.
PZ7.M5748Kasn   1991
    [Fic]—dc20   91-12768
                                                                                              CIP
                                                                                              AC

Printed in the United States of America.

Chapter 1

Zipper Troubles

Katie looked at the dress lying on her bed and sighed happily. It was perfect, absolutely perfect! And expensive! She picked up the scissors and cut off the price tag.

"This dress is now *mine*," she declared, holding it up and dancing in front of the mirror. As she moved it shimmered with deep blue and black and bits of gold.

In just a few hours, Katie's family would be going to a very important dinner honoring Katie's father, John McAbe Thompsen. Mr. Thompsen, a world famous correspondent, had visited many countries to gather material for his news stories. Whenever possible, he liked to take Katie and her brother Peter along on his traveling adventures.

All that morning Katie and her mother had been shopping for just the right dress for the dinner. It had gotten to be quite a pain after a while because they couldn't agree on what looked best.

Whenever Katie found something she liked, her mother would say, "No, no, that's completely inappropriate!" And whenever Mrs. Thompsen liked something, Katie would say, "No way! I'd rather die than wear that dumpy dress!"

But finally, just when they were ready to give up, Katie spotted the perfect outfit hiding on a rack behind the sales counter.

Mrs. Thompsen thought it looked too grown-up. "But it is very pretty, and seems to fit you perfectly," she said when Katie tried it on. "I'm so exhausted. I can't imagine looking any further. I suppose we'll have to buy it."

"Y-e-e-s!!" Katie cried. A few minutes earlier she had been so out of sorts, but now she hugged her mom and pronounced her the most wonderful mother in the world.

Back home, Katie rushed upstairs and undid the box. "Bee-yootiful," she sighed a she laid the gown on the bed. Just then there was a sharp rap on the bedroom door and in burst Beth McKinney, Katie's best friend.

"I came as soon as you called," gasped Beth. "Let me see—oh, it's gorgeous!"

Katie pulled the crisp material over her head and swished back and forth. She sat on the bed and crossed her legs gracefully.

"No one would ever know you were 10 years old. You could pass for at least 16," Beth said.

"Seriously?"

"Seriously!"

Katie gave a toss of her ponytail and looked in the mirror. "The question is, what to do with my hair. This dumb old ponytail has got to go."

"Maybe your mom could fix it in a French braid," Beth suggested.

"Great idea! French braids are in all the fashion magazines."

When Katie started taking the dress off Beth asked eagerly, "Can I try it on?"

Katie hesitated, taking longer than necessary to pull it over her head. Although both girls were the same age, Katie was tall and skinny, and Beth was shorter and . . . well, not exactly chubby, but not skinny either. Katie didn't want to hurt her friend's feelings, but she didn't really want her trying on the dress.

"I'm not sure if you should . . ." Katie began. Seeing Beth's hurt expression, she added quickly, "But I guess it's okay."

Beth managed to get the dress on without difficulty. "Here, can you zip it up?"

Katie carefully slid the zipper up halfway. "I don't think it'll go any farther."

"That's silly," said Beth. She pulled away from Katie and started fiddling with the zipper.

"Hey, stop it!" Katie cried.

But Beth decided to give one last yank. The zipper shot all the way to the top. "See?" she said with satisfaction. "It doesn't even feel tight."

Katie stood still, a look of horror frozen on her face. Then suddenly she exploded. "It's broken—you broke the zipper! My dress is ruined!"

Beth turned pale. "I—I didn't. I mean, I didn't mean to..."

"You—you—you...Uuuhh!! Take it off!" Katie screeched.

Close to tears, Beth removed the dress while Katie ran to find her mother. When Mrs. Thompsen and her daughter returned, Beth was gone.

"Look," Katie sobbed, holding up the dress. "She wouldn't even listen to me. She just kept forcing the zipper. Beth will never be my best friend again!"

"Katie Thompsen, don't you say such a thing. I'm surprised at you," her mother chided. She put her arm around Katie gently. "I know you're angry and disappointed, but remember how terrible Beth is feeling right now, too. Give me the dress, and I'll do my best to fix it before tonight."

Repairing the zipper wasn't easy. The material was delicate, and it was difficult to remove the tiny stitches holding the broken zipper in place.

The minutes ticked by until it was time to go. Mrs. Thompsen sighed and got up from the sewing machine. "I'm sorry, Katie. There just isn't enough time. You'll simply have to make the best of it and wear your green dress."

Wear that ugly old thing hanging in the hall closet that smelled like mothballs? A strangled moan escaped from Katie's throat. Her wonderful evening had been ruined. And it was all Beth's fault!

Standing by the front door ready to leave, Katie was a lump of misery. The green dress was too short and felt tight under the arms. Her long legs stuck out like sticks.

As Mr. Thompsen was about to lock the door, the telephone rang.

"Oh dear, now we'll be late," Mrs. Thompsen said.

But Katie's father was already hurrying back. "It might be important," he said over his shoulder.

"Yeah, maybe they've canceled the dinner," Katie muttered. "Then I wouldn't have to continue this horrible experience." She knew she shouldn't feel sorry for herself, but she couldn't help it.

It was a few minutes before Mr. Thompsen returned. Quickly he jumped in the car and they were off. Poor Katie stared out the window, ignoring the rest of her family. In the front seat her parents talked quietly.

Suddenly Peter nudged her. "Hey, I know this is the worst day of your life, but did you hear what Dad just said to Mom?"

Katie didn't answer.

Peter frowned. "Just thought you'd want to know—you're missing an interesting conversation."

Although she wouldn't admit it, Katie's curiosity was aroused and she leaned forward to listen.

"...I can't believe it," Mrs. Thompsen was saying. "Your father?"

"That's right. He wanted to congratulate me. After all these years..."

Katie forgot her troubles. Her father's father? That would be—

"Our *grandfather*?" she whispered to Peter in disbelief.

He nodded. "That's right! Grandpa disappeared years ago—and now he calls, out of the blue!"

"We've never even met him. Why...I thought he was...dead!" Excitement made Katie's stomach turn sommersaults. Many times she'd wondered about her grandfather...what he looked like, if he was nice or mean, unusual or ordinary...above all, why he had vanished so mysteriously all those years ago. Maybe she'd find out at last!

Chapter 2

Potatoes and Bombs

The dinner party was wonderful. So wonderful, in fact, that Katie forgot all about her dumpy green dress. She and her family sat at a round table in the center of the room with another journalist who was being honored as well. Her name was Rachel MacAbee. She was a tiny gray-haired woman who seemed to have visited every country in the world at least 10 times each. Oh, the stories she could tell! During World War II, she had been on the front line with the troops as a reporter.

"Nowadays that's not unusual for a woman. But back then—my goodness, it was unheard of!" she told them. Katie watched as the little lady ate her roast beef. It was hard to imagine Miss MacAbee doing anything more exciting than knitting in front of her television!

Katie listened intently as the journalist talked about her past adventures. During the war with Iraq, she'd almost been killed by a bomb explosion. To illustrate the noise, she clapped her hands together and yelled "Kerpow!" At the same moment Katie jabbed a round, slippery boiled potato with her knife. Whoosh! Like a deadly missile, a potato fragment flew across the table and landed with a splat in Miss MacAbee's hair.

Katie was horrified. "Oh, I'm so sorry!" she gasped.

Miss MacAbee laughed as she removed the mushy wad. "We pause to bring you an important news flash—Yes!—the potato-missile hit its target, but it didn't explode!

I've now survived *two* dangerous bomb attacks in my life!"

Becoming suddenly serious, she looked around the table. "It's good to laugh some-times, even about horrible things, but don't ever forget that war and bombs cause terrible suffering. It's *not* a laughing matter."

When Mr. Thompsen went up to accept his award for outstanding journalistic achieve-ments, his family applauded loudly. And when Miss MacAbee joined him to receive her award, the audience stood up as they clapped.

Back home that night, Katie jumped into bed tired but happy once more. In the dark she saw the outline of her new dress hanging on the closet handle. She was sorry she hadn't been able to wear it. Still, everything had turned out just fine.

As she closed her eyes, the sight of Beth yanking on the zipper flashed through her head. Katie felt unhappy all over again. She wasn't quite ready to forgive her friend yet. "Maybe tomorrow," she sighed sleepily. "Beth deserves to suffer a little. She should *never* have done that!"

The next morning brought some real surprises, and thoughts of Beth and the broken zipper were forgotten. A package had arrived with presents in it for everyone. During breakfast, Mr. Thompsen passed out the gifts.

"They're from your grandfather. I know you've never met him, but that seems likely to change."

Katie and Peter opened their gifts eagerly. Both received miniature sailing ships, exact copies of the one Captain Cook sailed around the world in during the 17th century. They were hand-carved from wood and beautifully painted.

"Your granfather made those tiny ships himself," Mr. Thompsen explained. "He's a fine woodcarver."

"Can you tell us about him?" Katie asked.

Katie and Peter waited expectantly. Their father sat down beside them and

Mrs. Thompsen did, too. She gave her husband's hand a reassuring squeeze.

"We have some wonderful news," she told the children.

"Yes, we do, Mr. Thompsen continued. "As you know, about 11 years ago, before either of you were born, your grandfather disappeared. It was shortly after your grandmoother died. I'm not really sure what happened—I think maybe he got mad at the world."

"Mad at the world?" repeated Katie. "He must have *really* been angry!"

"He was always a bit rough and wild, but with a heart of gold. He came from Australia originally. The last I heard of him, he was sailing around the South Pacific. And then he disappeared," Katie's father said.

Mrs. Thompsen continued the story. "You know we've never stopped praying for Grandpa all these years. And now it seems our prayers have been answered!"

Mr. Thompsen smiled and nodded. "That's right. Last month I received a letter from him—and I'm telling you, it almost gave me a heart attack! He wrote telling me where he lived and asking us to please come and visit. I could hardly believe it was true, but your mother and I started making preparations for the trip. We kept it a secret because we didn't want to disappoint either of you if it didn't work out. Well, last night I received a phone call—the first time I've heard my father's voice in over 11 years! And today this package arrived. It seems your grandfather really is serious and wants to see his family at last."

"So that means we get to visit him?" Katie asked excitedly.

"Where does he live?" asked Peter, "Utah, Arizona, New York?"

Mr. Thompsen laughed. "No . . . someplace quite different. Your grandfather lives on the tiny island of Tutuila in the South Pacific. The island is part of American Samoa, which means you'll find lots of things to remind you of home. The town he lives near is called Pago Pago."

Katie shook her head in disbelief. "A town called Pago Pago, in the middle of the South Pacific, and my grandpa lives there?"

"That's right," said Mrs. Thompsen. "Your

grandfather, Jake Thompsen, has always been...uhmm, well...unusual. He never really liked big cities, or crowds, or modern comforts."

Katie and Peter were both speechless.

Mr. Thompsen got up from the table. "Anyway, everything is arranged for us to leave the day after tomorrow. You're going to love the South Pacific, or Polynesia as it's also called. Close your eyes and picture swaying palm trees, white sandy beaches, blue skies, blazing sunsets, and sparkling turquoise water. That's exactly what Tutuila Island is like!"

Mrs. Thompsen didn't look entirely happy. "Of course you know about my concerns," she said to her husband. "I mean, your father is a wonderful man, but as I recall, he always seemed to be getting into trouble."

"I know, but I really feel we should go," said Mr. Thompsen. "It might be the children's only chance to get to know their grandfather."

Katie and Peter filled their suitcases with shorts and T-shirts and swimming suits—and lots and lots of suntan lotion.

"You'll be living in your swimming suits," said Mrs. Thompsen. "And you'll probably never even wear your shoes."

Katie waited until her mother had inspected her suitcase to make sure she'd included everything she needed. Then she closed her bedroom door and quickly added her new dress. The zipper had finally been replaced and Katie couldn't bear to leave it behind. She hoped her mother wouldn't mind too much if she brought it along "We might be living in our swimming suits," she told herself, "but I'll find a chance to wear this dress!"

Katie knew she should call Beth. She hadn't heard a peep from her friend since the disaster with the zipper. Each of them wanted the other to make the first move, and they were both hoping they wouldn't have to be the one to do it! But since Katie was about to leave, she realized it was up to her. Beth didn't even know the good news about her grandfather. It would be terrible to leave on such an exciting trip without telling Beth about it and saying good-bye.

Katie gathered her nerve and picked up

the telephone. Nervously she dialed Beth's phone number.

"Hello, Katie," said Mrs. McKinney. "Just one moment and I'll get Beth."

Katie waited . . . and waited . . . and waited.

Finally she heard a voice on the other end, but it wasn't Beth's. "I'm sorry, Katie," said Mrs. McKinney, "but Beth doesn't seem to be here. I think she's out riding her bike. Can you try again later?"

Katie tugged hard on her ponytail. What if Beth really was there, but didn't want to talk to her?

"No, I can't try later," she said loudly. "If Beth wants, she can call me. But that might be difficult because tomorrow I'll be gone!"

Katie hung up and ran to her room. She got out her diary and began to write,

> I tried to make up with Beth, but it didn't work. I'm sure she's home and just doesn't want to talk to me. It's not my fault. I tried to make it better, but she's being impossible. Well, I've got other things to think about—a wonderful trip to the South Seas and a visit with my grandpa.

That evening Katie tried to read a book about the South Seas, but she had a hard time concentrating. Every time the telephone rang she jumped up, expecting it to be Beth.

"What's gotten into you, Katie?" her mother asked. "You're acting like a jumping bean. Settle down!"

Katie stared at the pages in front of her. She was supposed to be reading about the voyages of the explorer Captain Cook. Hundreds of tiny islands dotted the Pacific, each one an unspoiled paradise. When the islands were discovered by Captain Cook and other explorers, many artists and writers and wealthy people went to live there, giving up the comforts of Europe and America for the simplicity of the South Seas.

"What's the book about?" Peter asked, looking over her shoulder. "Oh, Captain Hook—the pirate! There must have been lots of pirates back then. I wish there still were."

"Don't you know anything, Pete? Katie asked in disgust. "It's not about Captain *Hook*—he wasn't real. It's about Captain *Cook*, and he wasn't a pirate!"

Peter shrugged and opened his mouth in a huge yawn. "Big deal!" he said, and wandered off to bed.

Katie went to her room with a heavy heart. Why hadn't Beth called? There was only one explanation—Beth was ignoring her. Katie couldn't remember a time when the two hadn't been friends. They'd met on the first day of kindergarten and had been together ever since.

"Please, dear God, let everything be okay," Katie prayed. "And take care of us on our trip tomorrow," she added.

Chapter 3

Grandpa Thompsen

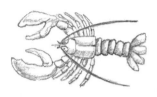

The next morning there was no time to even think about calling Beth. Dressed in flowered shirts, shorts and tennis shoes, the Thompsens boarded their flight for Hawaii. From there they would take a plane to an island called Upolu.

"Upolu is part of Western Samoa," Mr. Thompsen explained. "From there we fly, or take a boat, to Tutuila Island, which is in American Samoa. If it seems like a long journey, just remember what it would have been like to sail all that way in the old days!"

On the plane Katie rummaged through her bag, making sure she had everything. Her pocket New Testament was right on top, along with her sunglasses, chapstick, suntan lotion, her hat, her book about Captain Cook and, of course, her diary. Wait a minute . . .

She felt around inside, expecting to touch the familiar cover of the diary with its special lock. But she couldn't find it! Katie was sure she'd put it in yesterday. Or had she? No, now she remembered! Last night she'd taken it out again and written in it just before going to bed.

"Oh no—I can't believe it!" Katie wailed. "It's supposed to be here, but instead it's *there*! We'll have to go back!"

Mrs. Thompsen looked at her daughter in surprise. "Whatever are you talking about?"

"My diary! It's lying on my nightstand!"

"Oh, *of course* we'll have to go back," Peter mimicked with a grin.

"Is that all," her mother said with relief. "I thought you'd forgotten your entire suitcase or something."

Mr. Thompsen patted Katie's shoulder. "I know how important that diary is, but you'll just have to make do with a pad of paper. You can transfer it in when you get back."

"But it won't be the real thing," grumbled Katie. "It won't be—what's the word? Spontaneous. I like being spontaneous when I write."

Mrs. Thompsen raised her eyebrows in surprise. "Honestly, where do you get such ideas?"

"Now Katie," said her father, "I think it's time we had a little talk."

"Uh-oh," Katie said.

"I know how curious you are and how you love to find things out and write about them in your diary. And I know you're anxious to discover why grandpa disappeared and hasn't kept in touch all these years. We'd all like to find out. But just this once *please* control your curiosity! Don't ask embarrassing questions the minute we arrive. When Grandpa's ready, he'll explain it to us."

In Hawaii the Thompsens barely had enough time to race from one plane to the next. Before long they were airborne again, heading for the town of Apia on Upolu Island, somewhere in the vast blue ocean below.

Peter sat next to Katie, reading a book on pirates.

"Listen! The greatest pirate in history was Sir Henry Morgan. He didn't just rob strangers, he even robbed his friends! He hid a pile of treasure on a deserted island and some shipwrecked people found it in a cave. They got rescued and went home richer than kings!"

Katie's eyes sparkled. "I bet there's loads of undiscovered pirate treasure just waiting for us to find it!"

Her father laughed. "Actually, there are still pirates who sail around Indonesia and the South Seas robbing ships. Long ago the English called them Bogies. That's where we get the word for the scary bogie-man, which we still use today."

"Wow!" said Peter. "A real-life bogie-man-pirate. I'd like to meet one!"

Mr. Thompsen shook his head. "No, you wouldn't. They'd steal your money and slit your throat. And if you didn't have any money, they'd slit your throat anyway."

"Not a very nice bunch," his mother added.

Peter was disappointed. "Okay, maybe we should stay away from pirates. But I still think they're neat."

"Your attention, please. We are beginning our descent to Upolu," came the steward's voice. "Make sure your seatbelts are fastened and tray tables are in the upright and locked position. Thank you."

"Do you think Grandpa will be there to meet us?" Katie wondered.

"I don't think so. It's a long way for him to come," her father answered. Katie noticed his foot bouncing up and down and his fingers nervously drumming the seat.

The plane descended over a sparkling sea and touched the ground, screeching to a halt. A portable stairway was wheeled up to the door and everyone filed out. Katie stepped off

the stuffy plane into dazzling sunshine.
A slight breeze tickled her cheeks as
she breathed the sweet air. She had a
wonderful feeling she was going to love it
here!

Before long they were through customs
control and out of the tiny airport. Katie's
father scanned the faces of the people outside.
All at once, he looked intently.

"There he is," he said softly. "That's my
father."

Now Katie saw who he was looking at—
a man of about 70, tall and sturdy. His hair
was a dazzling white, from the top of his
head to the tip of his bushy beard. His tanned
skin looked like old cracked leather. He tilted
from side to side as he walked, like a sailor
who felt more at home on the rolling sea than
on dry land.

It was an awkward moment when Father
and son met for the first time after so many
years. No one quite knew what to say or do!
But at last the two men reached out and
hugged each other. After that everyone was
talking and laughing and hugging Grandpa
Thompsen.

"Careful there!" laughed the old man. He carried an armful of flower necklaces, or leis as they were called, and didn't want them to get squashed. Now he placed one around each of their necks and smaller ones on their heads. The leis were made from orchids, and smelled heavenly.

"A special custom in these parts," he said in a deep, rumbly voice. "A sign of hospitality and good will."

"I can't tell you how happy I am that you've come," he continued, leading them to a waiting taxi.

"We're so pleased you asked us," said Mrs. Thompsen.

Out of the corner of her eye, Katie watched her father as they rode into the town of Apia. It seemed as if a million thoughts were buzzing through his head. She tried to imagine what it would be like not to have seen her father for so many years and then suddenly have him re-appear. Why in the world had her grandfather disappeared anyway?

"Well, I intend to find out!" Katie thought. Then she remembered her father's orders. "Ooops! I guess I'll just have to control my curiosity!" she told herself.

Grandpa Thompsen took the family to Aggie's Hotel. He seemed to know everyone in the lobby, and Aggie Grey herself came to greet them. She was an ancient lady, part Samoan and part Scottish. A pink orchid was stuck into her dyed yellow hair.

"Why, Jake Thompsen, whatever are you doing in town?" she asked, beaming happily at Grandpa.

"This is a special occasion, Aggie," Grandpa replied. "My family just arrived.

28

Even an old badger like me comes out of his hole on a day like this!"

He picked up their two big suitcases in his strong hands and led them up the old stairs to their rooms. "Aggie's Hotel is pretty famous in these parts. I think you'll enjoy your stay here for the night. By bedtime you'll probably be ready for a good sleep. And Aggie's has the best beds in town!"

He shuffled awkwardly from one foot to the other, looking uncomfortable. "I'd like to stay and talk, but I have some repairs to make on my boat before morning," he said.

"You have your own boat?" cried Katie. She imagined herself sailing into the sunset, unknown adventures ahead!

"Can we see it?" asked Peter.

Grandpa pulled on his prickly beard, looking even more uncomfortable than before. "No, no, I don't think so. Not tonight. But I'll be back bright and early tomorrow to take you on board. Then we sail for Pago Pago!"

He walked over to Katie's father and gave him another hug. "It's great to see you again; it really is. I just need some time to get used to it. You see, I've been alone for so long . . ."

"We understand," Mr. Thompsen said.

Grandpa Thompsen looked relieved.
"Yes, well, uh . . . g'day, then."

The Thompsens watched as he disappeared down the stairs.

"Don't mind ol' Jake and his strange ways," said Aggie, huffing up the stairs with a pile of fresh white towels. "He has a hard time in company. You got to take him as he is, or not at all."

Mrs. Thompsen was feeling more nervous than ever. She had not expected they would sail all the way to Tutuila Island on Grandpa Thompsen's boat. "Oh dear, oh dear" she thought to herself. "Something's sure to go wrong!"

Aggie gave the Thompsens directions to a restaurant down by the harbor. "If you want tasty fish, fresh from the sea, it's the place to go."

When they arrived for dinner, the sun was just setting beyond the water. Palm trees swayed like hula dancers and sailing boats gently bobbed in the harbor.

The waiter seated them outside on a veranda overlooking the harbor. Next to their table was a tank filled with big pink lobsters. There were so many of them that they crawled on top and underneath each other, pinchers snapping and tentacles waving. To Katie, it looked as if each lobster was stuck to the next—like a long chain, or a necklace. "I wouldn't want to have *that* around my neck!" she thought.

Peter pressed his nose against the glass in fascination.

"A lobster dinner for you, Peter?" asked his father.

Mrs. Thompsen shuddered. "I hope not. To cook them, they put the lobsters in boiling water while they're still alive."

Katie was horrified. "That's disgusting! They may only be lobsters, but that's no reason to torture the critters!"

Peter sat back down. "No thanks, Dad. Uh... I'll try something else."

"How about squid... or octopus?" their waiter suggested.

Katie and Peter both winced at the thought.

In the end, a huge platter of different kinds of fish was chosen to share between them, along with an enormous plate of french fries and a green salad.

"If we get grossed out by the fish, at least we can eat the french fries," Peter said.

"I'll make a deal with you," said their dad. "If you each try *one* squid, you can have as much dessert as you want. But if you don't—then no dessert!"

Katie took a deep breath and placed a fried squid in her mouth. Slowly she bit down on the crunchy creature.

An unexpected smile spread across her face. "I can't believe it—it's great!" And she piled more on her plate.

"Leave some for the rest of us!" Peter said after he too had tried one.

Katie looked out across the harbor and spotted a familiar figure. "Hey, isn't that Grandpa?" she mumbled, her mouth full of french fries.

Sure enough, it was. Grandpa Thompsen had just hopped on board a sail boat. It looked older than he was, but just as sturdy.

"Where's he going, and why wouldn't he have supper with us?" Peter wondered as the boat began to move out of the harbor.

"He's probably just sailing out a bit, away from the noise and bustle," Mr. Thompsen explained. "Let's give Grandpa a chance to get used to having us here. I'm sure in time

he'll begin to feel more comfortable. I'm glad
you'll get to know your grandfather at last,
children. There's no one else quite like him."

Katie watched thoughtfully as the boat
sailed away. It almost seemed as if Grandpa
Thompsen was afraid to be with them because
of the questions they might ask. What was he
hiding? And what an interesting character he
was! She could hardly wait to jump on his
boat and sail to Pago Pago. She felt sure that
soon she would discover what had kept them
apart for so long.

Chapter 4

Stormy Seas

A leisurely stroll through Apia's narrow side streets ended the Thompsens' evening. Everything was dark except for the soft light of the street lamps. Katie imagined what the town must have been like back in the days of Captain Cook. There would have been no tourists wearing shorts and T-shirts and snapping pictures! Only the golden brown Polynesians. And of course there would have been lots of explorers and adventurers—and pirates!

Katie was so happy day-dreaming, she didn't notice she'd been caught up in a noisy bunch of tourists. When they'd passed, she found herself alone. Her family was nowhere to be seen. Where could they have gone? Katie's sandals tapped loudly as she ran to look down the next street. But no, it was empty, too.

How suddenly the silence had come! Only a minute before, the street had been filled with people. And now . . .

Katie heard footsteps behind her and turned quickly. Three large, dark shapes had come around the corner and were walking toward her on the lonely sidewalk. "Mom, Dad, Peter?" she whispered hopefully. But she knew better. The shapes and low, growly voices and rough laughter. One of them walked with a limp. Thoughts of bloodthirsty, one-legged pirates with patches over their eyes and pistols at their sides filled Katie's head. She turned and ran—right smack into another dark shape! It grabbed her and wouldn't let go.

"Help!" she screamed.

"Katie! Calm down!" said a familiar voice. She looked up into the welcome face of her father. Behind him was her mother and Peter.

"I thought you'd lost me! I got scared . . ."

She looked behind her. The frightening shapes were gone. Instead there was another group of laughing tourists disappearing in the distance.

Katie shook her head to clear her fuzzy brain. "I must have been imagining things. That long plane ride, and all that fried squid, *and* that giant chocolate sundae! I feel terrible."

Mrs. Thompsen gave her a big hug. "You need to snuggle down in that comfy bed and get some sleep. I think we all need to."

The next morning, Katie's scare seemed like just a bad dream, especially when she jumped on board Grandpa Thompsen's wonderful boat. It had a large, cream-colored sail and the name *Isabella* written on the side. "Named after your grandmother," Grandpa explained. Beneath the deck was one room with four bunks, a small stove and a tiny bathroom.

"What more could you ask for?" Grandpa said happily.

He squinted up at the sky. "Wind should be good. Weather'll be fair, too. Not quite hurricane season yet."

Mrs. Thompsen gasped. "Did you say *hurricane?*"

"Oh! Not to worry! They don't start for another three weeks or so."

Katie's mother looked longingly at a big, fancy luxury liner cruising out of the harbor. How she wished her family was safely on board, instead of sailing off in a matchbox!

"Now Julia, where's your spirit of adventure?" Mr. Thompsen whispered in her ear. "You won't find a better sailor than my old dad."

"Your old dad might be a wonderful sailor, but he has a bad habit of getting into trouble!" she whispered back.

Soon the wind had filled the sails and they were off. A brisk breeze pushed them out of the harbor and into the open sea. They watched as the emerald island of Upolu grew smaller and smaller, until it was only a speck on the horizon.

"Look!" cried Katie excitedly. Dolphins had appeared alongside the boat, jumping and chattering and shaking their long noses playfully. A beautiful milky white bird called a tern flew overhead, dipping and rising on the wind.

"I think it's racing our boat," laughed Peter.

Grandpa cooked lunch and dinner on his tiny stove and spent hours telling them old island tales.

"Do you know, according to Samoan myths, the first miracle of creation was fragrance?"

"I can understand why," said Mrs. Thompsen. "I've never seen so many flowers or smelled such wonderful aromas. Upolu was filled with them!"

"The people on the islands love to tell stories," he went on to explain. "The very highest honor a Samoan can have is to be called Tusitala, which means Teller of Tales. But very few of these wonderful stories have been written down. They're passed on from one generation to the next in songs and dances, or told in the evenings when the work is done."

That night the gently rolling sea rocked Katie to sleep. Only Grandpa Thompsen awoke shortly before dawn, sensing a change in the weather. He went up on deck and watched gravely as black clouds gathered over a dark, angry sea.

Suddenly, Katie was awakened out of a sound sleep to find herself being thrown out of her bunk and onto the floor. It took her a moment to realize what was happening. A storm! The words stuck in her throat. She tried to get up, only to be flung down again. "Whoah!" she cried as she slid across the floor and crashed into Peter's bunk.

By this time everyone was wide awake and holding onto the sides of their beds for dear life.

"I knew it," moaned Mrs. Thompsen, looking quite green and wild. "We should never have sailed in this matchbox!"

The noise of the storm was terrifying. From above came a sickening snap, like a giant tree breaking, then a loud bang. Katie screamed. Peter groaned and threw up, fortunately into the fish bucket.

Katie was sure they would drown. The boat would keel over and down they would go, down to the bottom of the sea. Sharks would pick their bones, leaving them clean and white. Her teeth chattered and her body shook.

Of course Beth would hear the news of their terrible tragedy. After Katie was dead and buried in the sea, would Beth forgiver her for being so mean about the dress? In the middle of that awful storm, in the middle of the ocean, Katie saw how silly and unimportant their argument had been.

"Please, dear God, bring us home safely," she prayed through her tears. "And please forgive me for being so horrible to Beth. And please, *please* bring me home so I can tell her I'm sorry!"

"I'm going on deck to help Grandpa," said Mr. Thompsen, opening the latched door in the ceiling.

Immediately, wind and rain rushed into the cabin. Grandpa's face appeared in the opening.

"Don't come out!" he yelled. "Nothing you can do!" He banged the door down again.

The family huddled together and prayed silently for a miracle.

Before long the door opened again and Grandpa Thompsen fell down the stairs, bringing a flood of water with him. He secured the latch and took off his rain coat and hat.

"Nothing more to be done for the moment," he said. "Can't get through on the radio. Doubt anyone could rescue us in this gale anyway. All we can do is ride out the storm and let it drive us where it will."

All day long the storm raged on. Everyone except Grandpa Thompsen took turns throwing up in the bucket. Sometimes they didn't quite hit the target. Katie almost wished she could die. Never had she felt so small and lost. Outside the dark cabin the wind howled and boards creaked and shuddered. Wave after giant wave picked up

the tiny boat and slammed it down again.
Up and down, up and down . . . Katie
thought it would never end.

It must have been late afternoon when
Katie finally fell asleep. She awoke to find
herself lying on the ground, and at first she
couldn't remember what had happened. Too
weak to get up, she listened to the sounds
around her. It was wonderfully quiet, and the
boat rocked gently from side to side. The
storm had passed!

Chapter 5

Pirates!

Katie hurried up on deck as fast as her wobbly legs could carry her. She was met by glaring sunshine and a flat, glassy sea. The boat was a mess! The main mast had been snapped in half and thrown into the waves. Only a jagged, splintery stump remained. At least the smaller mast hadn't been destroyed. Grandpa Thompsen was busily repairing a torn sail while her father helped.

The old man looked around at the unhappy family. "I guess it's all my fault, and I'm sorry," he told them gruffly. He frowned and stuck out his chin stubbornly. "But the forecast said clear weather. That storm came out of nowhere."

Mr. Thompsen shaded his eyes and looked across the still water. "And it seems to have disappeared into nowhere."

"Not to worry!" said Grandpa brightly.

Mrs. Thompsen groaned. When it came to adventures with Grandpa Thompsen, that was exactly what she *ought* to do, she thought to herself.

"I got you into this mess and I'll get you out of it," he promised. "As soon as we get a bit 'o wind, this sail'll carry us along just fine. It won't be speedy, but we'll make it."

Everyone joined in cleaning the deck. Then they went below to tackle the cabin.

"Yuck, it stinks down here!" said Peter, holding his nose.

"Buckets of throw up, and some on the floor," Katie said, feeling sick all over again.

But they had no choice except to get busy. "Unless you want to sleep with it like this tonight," said their mother.

"Never!" cried Katie and Peter.

It was an unpleasant job, but when it was done the cabin looked clean and tidy once more. They each finished off with a sponge bath, being careful to use as little water as possible.

"I'd give anything for a real shower or a bath," Katie thought longingly.

As night fell, a welcome breeze lifted the sail and the boat began to move. Everyone felt more cheerful. They sat on the deck and sang all the hymns and choruses they could think of that talked about Jesus calming the waters. They finally ended with "How Great Thou Art," sung at the top of their lungs!

Shortly before bedtime, Katie spotted a boat in the distance.

"Look, it's the first we've seen since the storm hit," she cried. It was nice to know there was someone else out on the lonely sea.

Silently they watched as the boat grew larger. "It's coming this way," said Peter.

"I hope it doesn't run into us," Mrs. Thompsen said anxiously. She imagined being crushed beneath its prow while up above tourists laughed and danced to lively music on the decks.

Grandpa Thompsen never took his eyes off the approaching boat. Suddenly he snuffed out the light. "Don't think we want to let them know about us. Sure wish old *Isabella* could move a bit faster!"

"Why'd you do that?" cried Mr. Thompsen. "They might run over us in the dark!"

"Better that, than to be captured by pirates!" Grandpa hissed.

He started pulling ropes and turning the sail. "I'll try to get out of its way. If not, when I give the signal, you be ready to send up the flare and turn on the lantern. And kids, get some pots and pans and start banging for all you're worth. That way, if we can't escape, at least we won't get crushed."

Quietly Grandpa Thompsen turned the sail and the boat picked up a little speed. "I think we just might make it," he said.

But he was wrong. A shout rang out and a bright light lit up the escaping boat. They had been discovered!

A loud voice yelled, "Eh!—what have we here? A boat tossed by stormy seas, by the look of it!" Several other voices joined in with lots of unpleasant laughter. Because of the bright, blinding light in their eyes, the Thompsens couldn't see the faces that went

with the voices. But one thing was certain—
they didn't sound friendly.

"Where were you sneaking off to in such
a hurry?" yelled another voice. "We'll just
have to come on board and say hello!"

"Now we're in for it," said Grandpa
Thompsen softly. "It's bogies—and in a nasty
mood by the sound of it. Listen, even if you
don't like 'em, be polite to the monsters.
They're a conceited bunch, on account of their
long and bloody history—all the way back to
the days of the first explorers. You leave the
rest to me, and we just might get out of this
alive. And hey!—not to worry!" he finished
brightly.

Mrs. Thompsen thought she'd faint. Not

to worry? Never in her entire life had she had a better reason to worry!

"Looks like you'll get your chance to see pirates, Pete," said Katie, her heart beating wildly.

"Yeah," squeaked her brother. He didn't sound at all happy about it.

Grandpa Thompsen scrambled into the cabin and out again. He winked at Katie and slapped his belt. "Got my trusty knife. They can search me upside down and inside out, but they'll never find it."

By this time, the larger boat was alongside Isabella. Loud, mean sailors with long knives and pistols swarmed on board and began searching everywhere. When they had finished, the cabin looked like a hurricane had hit it all over again.

The biggest, roughest sailor gave Grandpa Thompsen a shove and barked in his face. "Pretty slim pickin's. Not a penny on board! What's in your pockets?" He searched Grandpa and then Katie's father. Next he grabbed Mrs. Thompsen's purse.

"I'm afraid we only carry traveler's checks. N-n-no, no cash," she told him.

The pirate threw up his hands in disgust. She watched miserably as her purse sailed through the air and landed in the sea with a splash.

"What's the world coming to?" roared the pirate. "Don't nobody carry cash anymore?" He laughed loudly and the other pirates joined in. "You'll just have to come along with me. Our Captain'll want to speak to you."

The Thompsens were hoisted on board the bigger boat.

"It might look old and dirty, but wow!—this boat's fast," Grandpa Thompsen whispered to Katie. "It'll outrun any police patrol in these waters. And did you notice the flag? That's Thaddeus Blake's flag—Big Blake as he's called. And a meaner old sea dog you'll never meet."

"Big Blake'll see you now," said one of the pirates. He cleared his throat loudly and spat on the deck.

Yuck! Katie felt scared to death as they were led down the narrow staircase and into the Captain's quarters.

"My goodness, he's *BIG*," Katie thought when first she saw him. Big body, big belly, big beard, big teeth, big hands and feet, and absolutely the biggest, most booming voice she'd ever heard. Only his eyes were small, and black. When they saw Grandpa Thompsen, they opened in surprise. A smile spread from ear to ear.

"Well, well, well! If it ain't Jake Thompsen!"
A toothpick stuck out of the side of Big Blake's mouth, moving up and down as he spoke.

The Thompsen family watched in amazement as Grandpa hugged the pirate and cried

nervously, "Hey Thaddeus, you old sea dog! It's great to see you again!"

The Captain turned his big smile on the rest of the family. He even kissed Mrs. Thompsen's hand.

"This calls for a celebration. Pull up some chairs and join me for dinner!" He ordered the sailors to prepare a feast, acting as if he were captain of a luxury cruise ship, rather than a filthy old pirate's boat.

Soon a meal of oily fish and limp vegetables was placed on the table. The Captain put a dirty napkin on his lap and invited everyone to dig in.

"So tell me, Jake," he roared, food falling out of his mouth, "where you been all these long years?"

Grandpa Thompsen coughed and looked uncomfortable. "Oh, here . . . and there. I used to sail with Old Joe. You know, down south a ways . . ."

"Ahha! Old Joe, let me see . . . He's not been around since he took that pardon from the government—in fact, I guess he's *dead*." Thaddeus Blake looked at Grandpa with his tiny black eyes and gave a nasty laugh. "You wouldn't have accepted that pardon, now would you?"

Grandpa Thompsen seemed to be having trouble eating because he coughed and coughed. "Who, me? I'd never stop pirating, you know that! Like I said, I've been down south. Only now my family came to visit and I'm taking them to Pago Pago." He got up from the table. "In fact, it's been nice visiting with you, but we should be on our way."

Captain Blake pushed him down again. "Not so fast old friend!"

Katie's head ached. She was trying hard to think. Could it be that her very own grandfather was a pirate, or had been in the past? It sounded as if the Samoan government had offered the pirates a pardon if they promised to stop pirating. And it sounded as if Captain Blake killed anyone who accepted the pardon!

"I'll bet Grandpa and Old Joe accepted it," thought Katie. Old Joe was dead and Katie didn't like to think what might happen to them! She tried to swallow her rubbery vegetables, but quickly clutched her throat in a fit of coughing."

"My, oh my, everyone seems to be having trouble with their dinner!" cried Captain Blake. "We can't have you all choking to death!" He roared with laughter.

Chapter 6

Pago Pago at Last

"Ouch!" Katie cried as they were thrown into the dark storage room, the door locking behind them. Huddled together for comfort, the Thompsens stared at Grandpa.

He stared back. "Okay, okay. I guess it's time for an explanation."

"I guess it is," Mr. Thompsen said softly.

"I was going to explain everything to you eventually. I'm just sorry it had to come out like this," Grandpa began. "It all started a long time ago. Your mother Isabella—the children's grandmother—was ill and needed an operation. I started pirating to earn the money. But it was honest pirating, mind you, not like Thaddeus Blake! I never hurt anyone and I only stole from people who could afford it."

"Honest pirating?" cried Mrs. Thompsen. "There's no such thing! And there's no excuse for doing it!"

"I know," Grandpa said, hanging his head. "That's why when the government offered a pardon to the pirates who would stop, I jumped at the chance. The problem was, Captain Blake didn't like it and he went around killing anyone who accepted the pardon. That's how Old Joe died."

"So that's why you disappeared? To escape Captain Blake?" asked Katie.

"That's right. It was shortly after my dear Isabella died. She never knew I was a pirate; I'd hoped no one ever would. I thought I'd be safe now, and Captain Blake would have forgotten about me. After all, it's been 10 years since I accepted that pardon. But Big Blake has a long memory and a short temper! I so much wanted to see my grandchildren just once in my life. I'm an old man..." Poor Grandpa Thompsen seemed close to tears. "I guess it's true what the Bible says, 'Your sins shall find you out.'"

"Well, it's no good worrying about the past," said Katie's father. "What's important is that God forgave you, and we certainly do, too. You had no way of knowing all this would happen."

"At least we're together, Grandpa," Katie declared bravely.

Grandpa Thompsen sniffled. "Thank you. You can't imagine how much that means to me. I'm so sorry for putting you all in danger."

The sound of a key turning in the lock made everyone freeze and listen. The door opened slowly and a skinny old pirate tip-toed into the room. He put a finger to his lips and said "Shh."

"I don't know if you remember me, Captain Thompsen," he whispered, "but I sailed with you and Joe in the old days. You were always a kind captain and good to your crew. There's a few others on board who remember you, too, and we don't like the way Big Blake is treating you." He grinned widely. "We're going to help you escape!"

Grandpa Thompsen grinned back and slapped the little pirate on the back, almost knocking him down. "I sure do remember you. You're Bill Beeper! Well, what are we waiting for? Let's get out of here!"

Grandpa took off his wide belt and removed the knife from a slit in the leather. "I knew this would come in handy."

When he saw Mrs. Thompsen's shocked face he said quickly, "It's not to hurt anyone with, only to get them out of the way if I need to."

Bill Beeper led them quietly up the stairs and onto the deck. Everyone was asleep except for three pirates who were lowering a rope over the side. They turned and helped the Thompsens climb down to their boat.

Bill called softly, "Captain Blake'll sleep late tomorrow morning. With this breeze you'll reach Tutuila by sunrise and you'll be safe."

Thanking Bill and the three pirates, the Thompsens sailed off into the moonlit night. By 6 o'clock the next morning the welcome sight of land met their tired eyes. By seven, they had reached Pago Pago harbor. Katie and Peter jumped off the boat and nearly kissed the ground. It was wonderful to have reached dry land at last!

The first thing the Thompsens did was hurry to the police station and report what had happened. Then they picked up some groceries at the local market and took off in Grandpa Thompsen's old car. It had been parked down a side street waiting their return. How happy they were to be heading out at last for Grandpa's hide-away house, nestled on the edge of a sleepy lagoon.

"Most people on the island don't live in real houses, but I built one for myself," explained Grandpa. "Usually they live in what's known as a fale. It has a thatch or tin roof, supported by posts. Samoans don't care much about privacy because the fale doesn't have any walls! That's one thing I never could get used to—I wanted a house with walls and a bit of privacy!"

61

The Thompsens spent the next two weeks with Grandpa swimming in the sea, hiking in the hills, listening to his wonderful stories and occasionally going into town. They grew to know and love the old man and forgave him completely for his past mistakes. He certainly was quite a character and, as Mr. Thompsen had said, there was no one else quite like him.

Katie and Peter's favorite stories were the ones Grandpa told about his pirate days. Mrs. Thompsen wasn't quite sure she approved, but he was such a wonderful story-teller even she found herself listening on the edge of her chair. To Katie, his stories sounded a bit like Miss MacAbee's.

"She told us wonderful stories at a dinner we went to right before we left on our trip," Katie told her grandfather. "Some pretty horrible—and exciting—things had happened to her, too. But she was able to look back on her life with a sense of humor."

"That's a good thing to be able to do," said Grandpa Thompsen. "Where would we be if we couldn't laugh at ourselves once in a while? It also takes real courage to face past mistakes honestly and then move forward and learn from them. Believe me, I'm trying to do that right now!"

On Sunday, Grandpa invited them to the little church near his home. Katie removed her beautiful new dress from the suitcase and put it on. Finally she would be able to wear it! It seemed like an eternity since the last time she had tried it on. So much had happened since then!

Looking in the mirror, she thought about Grandpa Thompsen's words, "It takes courage to face your mistakes and learn from them." Slowly she took the dress off again and put it back in the suitcase.

"I won't wear it until I've asked Beth's forgiveness," she said to herself. How badly she wished she could tell her right now! But she would have to wait until she got home.

The booming of a huge log drum could be heard, calling the people to worship. Women in long white muumuus and men in jackets and wrap-around skirts, or lavalava as they are called, filed into the small building. All were careful to leave their shoes outside. The service reminded Katie of the ones back home. The choir even sang the song "Hallelujah!" which she knew well.

Afterward, the villagers had a feast of yams, taro root and chicken and corned beef, all cooked in a clay stove. It was a traditional Samoan meal, one their ancestors had served since the days of the explorers.

The village chief, Moelagi, greeted the Thompsens respectfully in the name of the whole village. Then he turned to Grandpa Thompsen.

"I have some wonderful news for you," he told him. "The police have captured Captain Blake and he's now in jail in Apia awaiting his trial. I don't think he'll be bothering us, or you, for a very long time—hopefully never again!"

When Grandpa Thompsen heard that, he gave a loud whoop and started dancing a jig.

"This calls for a celebration," he cried. Grabbing Katie, he twirled her across the grass. Soon everyone joined in.

The celebration lasted long into the afternoon, with games and songs and of course lots of story-telling. Beneath the swaying palms, wide-eyed children listened as

Grandpa Thompsen told the tale of their escape from the pirates. Over and over he repeated it, each time adding something more, until at last it was nothing at all like what had really happened!

"Now that's the worst case of exaggeration I've ever heard!" Peter whispered to Katie.

"I know," she answered. "But he sure can tell a great story! He's a real Tusitaulu— a Teller of Tales!"

The Thompsens returned to Grandpa's house with gifts of flowered lavalava for each of them and a beautifully woven mat for Mrs. Thompsen.

"It's too lovely to put on the floor," she said. "I think I'll hang it on the wall when we get home."

Home! The day quickly arrived when it was time to go. Tearfully, the Thompsens said their good-byes.

"Why don't you come with us?" Mr. Thompsen asked his father. "You don't have to hide out anymore."

Grandpa shook his head. "This is where I belong. It's my home."

"You're not going to disappear again, are you?" Katie asked anxiously.

"You wouldn't, would you?" Peter added with a worried frown.

Grandpa Thompsen gathered them up in his powerful arms. "Never, even in a million years! And I promise to visit as soon as possible. It's a long way to sail, but I'll enjoy it."

"Sail!" gasped Mrs. Thompsen. "You're not going to sail all the way to California!"

Grandpa looked surprised. "Of course I am! You won't catch me in an airplane!" He shuddered. "An unnatural way to travel! Ahh, but give me a boat and the open sea—that's the life for me!"

Katie thought she would never survive the long plane journey home, she was so anxious to see Beth! And even though she was exhausted when they finally arrived, the first thing she did was race down the street to find her friend. She hadn't gone far before she ran into Beth coming in the opposite direction."Oh!" the two girls cried, looking at each other.

"I just wanted to say—" they both started at once. Then they stopped talking and burst into laughter.

"Oh, Beth," cried Katie, hugging her friend. "You don't know how happy I am to see you. I've been shipwrecked, lost at sea, and captured by pirates, but all I could think about was how much I wanted to come home and say I was sorry. I should never have gotten mad about a dumb old zipper. There are so many more important things to think about!"

Beth's face lit up with happiness. "I'm so glad everything's okay. And I'm sorry too, for yanking on that silly zip. Let's just forget the whole thing."

"Good idea!" agreed Katie.

The two girls walked arm in arm down the street.

"So, tell me all about your trip," said Beth. "You said something about a shipwreck and pirates, but that's a joke, right?"

Katie laughed. "Are you kidding? You'll never believe what happened!"

Beth listened wide-eyed while Katie talked about her adventures. Then they ran into Katie's house and got her diary off her nightstand. "Let's go!" Katie said with a grin.

They headed out the door and skipped up the hill to the old oak tree behind the Thompsen's home. Sitting beneath the shady branches, Beth kept Katie company while she wrote everything down in her diary."It's important to remember all the details and to write it like it really happened," Katie said earnestly.

Her friend nodded. "I know, you've told me a thousand times! Someday your diary might be famous."

"*Might* be? It *will* be famous. I just know it!"

The two girls smiled happily, and Katie said, "Adventures in far away places are exciting, but there's nothing as great as being home again."

"You can say that again!" Beth declared.

So Katie did!

Dear Diary,

I can't believe it, but I only have a few more pages left in my diary. It's so full of traveling adventures, I guess I'll just have to buy a new one. Maybe my parents will get me one for my birthday!

Anyway, let's see, where should I start? When we took off for the South Seas, I never dreamed so many exciting things would happen. You always hear about how people go on holiday to the South Pacific because it's so relaxing. Well, there was nothing relaxing about our trip! I'm not sure which was scarier—the storm or being captured by pirates. Probably the storm was the worst because I got so sick and I didn't want to drown.

Beth and I have been having so much fun. We wrote a play all about my trip. Then we got Pete and his friend Jeff to help us do it. Beth and Jeff's parents all came over, and my Mom and Dad cooked hamburgers. After dinner we did the play. It was totally fantastic! The only problem was that we started laughing in the parts where it was supposed to be scary. We just couldn't help it! That meant that our parents started laughing, too. Finally everyone was laughing so hard we had to stop. But they said we did a good job anyway, and I think we did, too.

I'm glad Beth and I are friends

again. It was such a dumb old argument, all about a dumb old zipper. Dad says people usually argue about silly things that aren't important, and they refuse to forgive each other because they're too proud. I guess that's what happened to me and Beth. It's kind of like in the Bible where Peter asks Jesus how many times he should forgive his brother and Jesus says not just seven times, but seventy times seven times. Now that's a lot! Probably Beth and I will do more things to make each other mad in the future. I just hope we will always remember to forgive each other.

I miss my Grandpa. I really miss him a lot. But he says he'll come and visit next summer — if his boat will make it that far. Mom is already getting nervous. She says Grandpa attracts trouble like honey attracts bees! My poor Mom! She thinks her hair turned gray on our trip, though everyone keeps telling her it looks just the same.

Well, that's all for now — which is a good thing since this is the last page! The next time I write it'll be on the first page of a new diary. I can hardly wait!